Contents

NARCISA
AND
OTHER STORIES

LUIGI GUALDO (1844-1898) was born into a wealth family in Milan. He wrote poetry, short stories and novels, in both Italian and French, spent his time navigating between Italy and France, and associated with many of the most important writers of both countries. His works include: *Novelle* (1868), *Une ressemblance* (1873), *Un marriage excentrique* (1879), and *Decadenza* (1892).

BRENDAN and ANNA CONNELL have together translated numerous texts from Italian, including *Alcina and Other Stories* (Snuggly Books, 2019) by Guido Gozzano, and Ruggero Vasari's Futurist play *Raun* (Snuggly Books, 2023).

LUIGI GUALDO

NARCISA
AND
OTHER STORIES

TRANSLATED BY
BRENDAN & ANNA CONNELL

THIS IS A SNUGGLY BOOK

ISBN: 978-1-64525-155-2

Introduction

AMONG the numerous Italian writers who were active in the second half of the nineteenth century, Luigi Gualdo (1844-1898), the somewhat obscure and forgotten author of the stories in the present volume, is surely one of the most deserving of rehabilitation.

He was born in Milan. His father, Alessandro, was a wealthy landowner and his mother, Bianca Taccioli, the descendant of nobility. The family's wealth allowed Luigi to devote himself to study, with frequent visits to France.

He spent a good part of his childhood in Switzerland and England. In Milan his family had a substantial residence on the via Bagutta, and in Varese they maintained the

Villa Mirabello, which was the home inherited from his mother's side of the family, and which today houses the city's Archaeological and Civic Museum.

After graduating from high school, he enrolled at the University of Pavia, where he studied Law.

In the summer of 1865, while vacationing in Nice, he wrote his first short story, "La canzone di Weber" (translated in the present volume as "A Song by Weber").

In 1866, at the outbreak of the Third Italian War of Independence, he attempted to join Garibaldi's army, but was refused on account of epileptic seizures he suffered from.

In 1868 his first book, *Novelle*, a collection of short stories, was published, presumably at his own expense. This volume contained "La canzone di Weber" as well as the other two items in the present volume, "Narcisa" and "Una Scommessa" (translated as "A Bet").

It was in 1868, in fact, that he seemed to have decided to launch himself fully into a literary career, spending the latter part of that year, as well as the first months of 1869, in Paris, where he met numerous writers and became friends with Théophile Gautier, Paul Bourget, Stéphane Mallarmé, and François Coppée. Later, in 1872, he would translate Coppée's *Deux douleurs* into Italian.

In Italy he associated with Emilio Praga, Arrigo Boito, Giovanni Camerana, Giovanni Verga, and many others.

He wrote four novels, two in Italian, and two in French, as well as a collection of poetry, *Le Nostalgie* (1883), in Italian.

Gualdo, furthermore, became close to Robert de Montesquiou, (who is said to have been the model used by J.-K. Huysmans in that writer's masterpiece *À rebours*) as well as an intimate associate of Edmond de Goncourt and Émile Zola—influences which are especially obvious in his novels.

In 1893 an attack of epilepsy seriously undermined his health, and the next year his legs became paralyzed, presumably as a result of syphilitic myelitis, with which he had been diagnosed.

He died in Paris.

—Brendan Connell

NARCISA
AND
OTHER STORIES

Narcisa

SHE was more beautiful than it is possible to imagine. Setting eyes on her, one saw a compendium of every dream, of every aspiration; the highest and the most perfect ideal. She reconciled all visions: a poet of the North, who loved pale Ossianic figures, would have found her more complete than any of his creations, while a pagan worshipper of form would have declared her to be the most magnificent expression of woman. To a disciple of Phidias[1] she would have appeared as a Greek beauty; she would have fascinated Horace as much as Byron, both Rubens and Raphael, Gautier as well as Hugo. Passing the woman, it

---

1 Greek sculptor, c500-432 B.C.

was impossible not to turn around, astonished, and admire her.

It would have been very difficult to explain, physiologically, the mystery of this great beauty. Her parents were normal, but common, and certainly one would not have expected such a flower to have arisen from the tiny seed that was put in the earth. From her first days there was something unusual about the girl. When her mother saw in front of her that white little face,—completely surrounded by lace, with those two little arms of alabaster emerging from the swaddling-bands—along with the first joyful burst of maternal love at the sight of her own creature, there was united a feeling of admiration for the really perfect regularity, as much as it was possible, of those small features, for the myriad things that those little eyes were already saying.—While growing up she developed steadily in natural and irresistible grace. At five or six years of age, a more charming girl could not be imagined. At that age, when the desire to be admired has not yet arisen, she already instinctively dressed herself with a childish elegance far distant from other girls. She ran and jumped like the others; but each of her movements, each of her gestures, was harmonious.—She had something intense about her. She was neither pensive nor taciturn, as children often are when their intelligence develops prematurely; but she had a quality different from others, inexplicable and difficult to define. Mirrors had a strange influence on her. Every time she found herself in front of a mirror, she stopped and remained for a great while, motionless and enraptured by her own beauty.

Naturally all this, both her beauty and bizarre manner, increased. She went through all the stages of childhood, becoming more indifferent day by day towards that which shapes life at that period; and she reached sixteen years of age without her parents being able to notice in her any tendency, any predilection for a particular study or amusement. Her eyes were full of expression, and certainly she was not lacking in aptitude; but she was interested in nothing except those things which related to form, to material and external beauty, to the aesthetics of line and colour. In history, only the pagan ages fascinated her, or the mythological fables in which the cult of beauty was exalted. She searched for the sensitive side in all things; she preferred a fine statue to a fine painting, and a painting to the most enchanting music. She had no desire to be irreligious, but she understood little of the divine poetry of Christianity and certainly preferred the young Christ, handsome with the sweetest celestial beauty, with a forehead crowned by an aureole and surrounded by a nimbus of light, to the emaciated Christ, livid, thin and nailed to the cross of redemption, handsome only due to his faith and sacrifice. She instinctively understood art; she would remain absorbed for hours in mute contemplation before a Venus, a dream realised in marble.

When she read the story of those incomparable times when Phidias and Pygmalion flourished, she felt an irresistible attraction towards the arcades of Athens, with their serene architecture irradiated by the purest Greek sun; she would have liked to have run up the steps of the temples, among their white columns, or to have wandered around the woods which, in spite of the thickness of the verdant trees, were penetrated by that splendid light and illuminated by the reflection of a blue sky.

The first time that she was taken into society, to a ball, her appearance made such a great impression that for a whole month nothing was talked of but her. She was dressed in white, without ornaments, with nothing—nothing but the splendour of her eyes whose glance was magic, the pure beauty of her features, the poem of her figure. She was modest, but not timid; she did not lack spirit, and she knew how to converse, but how was it possible to sustain a conversation with her? The irrepressible admiration she aroused by her every gesture, by each of the most fleeting expressions of her face, by every movement of her body, distracted one to the point of being nearly unable to either listen or reply. If, while talking, she lifted a hand to put a disobedient ribbon back in its place, the sight of those white fingers, oblong and perfectly shaped, would make one lose the thread of what one was saying.

Meanwhile, though she did not manifest any particular predilection, still the physical and intellectual precocity of her childhood did not deny itself, and at that age she was already a woman. Her forehead was radiant with adolescence and every time she spoke, her voice, mysteriously harmonious, seemed to be singing the hymn of youth. Then she, the extraordinary maiden, like all others arrived at that point when the heart is moved by its first quiver, and, without making the smile of life's morning disappear, the first tear appears on the eyelash.

She arrived at that instant when the wind blowing through the branches, the breeze rippling the water's surface, the whisper of the evening, the song of the birds, all nature's light and potent murmuring becomes a single voice and speaks a single word; when the blue of the sky, the shiny outline of the clouds, the green of the leaves, the thousand warm and harmonious tints of the earth seem to blend into a single colour and are turned into a single sentiment. Yet nothing moved, nothing quivered within her.

One never saw a more perfect expression of the virgin; her unquestionable and almost insolent beauty still, however, was quite vague, her lovely figure, although complete, still indistinct—almost like a divine thought that was not yet fully manifest and a part of her still existed elsewhere. Also, it seemed impossible that she could become more beautiful. She thought almost continually about her own beauty and occupied herself with almost nothing else, but she did it in a way that is quite difficult to explain. She was not motivated by feminine coquetry or ambition; she acted with concentrated and distracted seriousness, as if out of necessity; she seemed to be obeying a command. Self-admiration and the feeling of beauty were in her like a divine instinct: it seemed that, by being thus occupied, she was fulfilling an office.

She spent long hours in front of the mirror and was never through with admiring herself and arranging her hair; but she did not hide it like the others, she did it in public, as if the worship of her own person was simply artistic, and, that is to say, impersonal.

It seemed that self-love excluded in her the possibility of another love. Her parents watched to see if, in that dangerous age in which she found herself, someone would make her heart palpitate for the first time or strike her imagination; but they noticed nothing and really there was nothing to be noticed. She met the most alluring young men, but for one reason or another, took to nobody. They noticed this almost with pleasure, because, if there were no preconceived sympathies to be overcome, they believed that it was easy for her to choose. They were very rich, rich enough to be permitted high aspirations. Such an occasion was not late to arrive. A young man, the last descendant of an illustrious family, which would become extinct upon his death, fell more deeply in love than anyone with the extraordinary beauty of the girl, and asked for her hand. He was rich, liked by everybody, of a good and loyal disposition and certainly not bad looking, though his appearance was common enough. She refused. Her father did not want to force her, but was much grieved by such a refusal, which he considered due to some unpardonable caprice. The same thing happened with twenty others.

A few years went by and, due to her obstinacy, she truly brought suffering to those who loved her. The idea of marriage she found repugnant. She had to undergo a strong internal struggle before comprehending that, in this world, it is not possible to be overly eccentric, and that she could not act so absolutely contrary to everyone else's will. But finally she understood that one has to make concessions, and told her father, thereby rendering him happy, that she would accept the hand of the first young man to present himself, provided this satisfied all those who had been for so long advising her to yield, and provided that she did not dislike the young man too much.

The first that dared to ask for her hand was Count R——, a man quite rich, reasonably in demand, and who had long been struck by her superb beauty.

She was faithful to her promise and accepted. She was then twenty years old.

Her beauty, which became more intense every day, was such that one who never had the good fortune to see her cannot even imagine. She acquired universal fame, and was spoken of from the palace of the court to the garret of the poor. Poets of every calibre sang of her in all metres, and painters, seeing her, set to work with brushes and palettes.

The Count was a handsome southern type, tall and well built; he had eyes and hair that were very black, and fine features. As to his character, he was quiet, with intelligence sufficient to his needs, rather insipid and quite indolent.

The marriage took place and was like all other marriages; it was followed by a brief journey like all other nuptial journeys, and a most typical honeymoon.

On her return, our heroine, who we can now call Countess, was very much changed. It seemed impossible, but it was as if she had become more beautiful. Her beauty had not changed character but it had become more splendid. A poet would probably have preferred her as before, but not a sculptor. Although nobody, whatever his taste, could remain insensible in front of her, her being the result of all dreams, as already said, still many—all those who search for the deep delicacies of the soul—would have found in her an indefinable but true shortcoming. We love human things; our fragility, our mistakes, our weaknesses, even some of our misfortunes; we are attracted to them and desire them, we love them as if they were virtues and not defects; we are composed partially of the supernatural and partially of the terrestrial, of something superb and of something low, yet still we love our clay as it is. In her there was a lack of imperfection, a lack of fragility. Painful and despairing, there was no possibility of love in her—it was a sublime frailty. She was too perfect and at times that perfection was oppressing and that supreme serenity gave pain. It was not possible to see where another's sentiments could have found place amidst that desolate calm, and her beauty seemed intangible and inaccessible.

Once married, she was obliged to play a more active role in the community, and appeared to be somewhat distracted from her habitual preoccupation. She lived more or less the same life as everyone else—she went into society and received company—but the study and love of self was always her principal concern. The women were not as jealous of her as might be supposed. First of all, it was useless to criticise her beauty, and secondly, they did not have much to fear from her because she did not come onto the field to fight and did not care to make use of her weapons.

But they wounded, and caused very grave injuries. We renounce telling of all the passions she excited, of all the evil she did, though certainly with the utmost innocence, because to do so would fill volumes. How many lovers cursed her, how many mothers, seeing her, felt their eyes swell with tears, and how many asked her for pity! How many attempts were made, in every way, to make the secret chords of her heart vibrate, to agitate the serene limpidity of her gaze! But she possessed the imperturbable calm of marble.

To those who reproached her for her insensitivity, and when talking of those who considered her to be a merciless woman, she would say:

"Look at me. How can you consider me wicked? What blame should be mine if I cannot live like others and if I have the good fortune not to suffer?"

And everyone remained struck by the radiant peacefulness of her face, dazzled by that invincible loveliness, while she pronounced these words which were full of superhuman tranquillity.

Often, rather strange scenes took place. The Countess received twenty letters a day—letters of love, entreaty, jealousy, fury and despair—which she threw into the fire without finishing.

The artists, the poets, the observers all occupied themselves with her as if she were a living enigma. The majority of them desired to know her, and as she had intelligence and spirit, her rooms were open to the aristocracy of genius and, naturally, the other aristocracies as well.

Her taste in art was exquisite, and of this her apartments were visible proof. Everything, from the vaulted ceilings, from the frames and the furniture, to the smallest object, had an artistic value. There were paintings chosen with subtle discernment from among the masterpieces of the best schools, statues which reminded one of the Greeks, vases from China and Japan, works of enamel and carvings, velvets and damasks which fell in majestic folds, Gobelin tapestries with colours exceedingly bright and harmonious, and, moreover, mirrors of every sort, from those which came from modern factories and stretched across entire walls to those small and very elegant mirrors of Venice, with frames slightly darkened by time, covered with twisted baroque ornamentation and gemmed with microscopically tiny mirrors. All these things were arranged with that order of sober elegance which indicates an artist's taste pushed to its ultimate consequences; the harmony of colours and forms, the difficult union of styles, were obtained with the infallible security of the hand of an expert. And it was her indeed who had presided over everything because, after having thought of herself, what was left for her to do but think about that which was around her? She instinctively loved beautiful things, and so reached that perfect knowledge of art which ordinarily is not acquired except after long study and minute observation; she had powerful intuition when it came to beautiful antiques, as if she had always busied herself with archaeology, and in an antique-shop she could tell at first glance what was worth buying.

Painters and sculptors asked for her opinion; one brought along two or three sketches so that she might decide which of them was better to undertake, another begged her to go to his studio so as to advise him on the attitude of a statue. And she always answered with surprising correctness and often her own eyes would see far beyond those of the artist. Many times she would say: "Do it like this," and the artist, though not persuaded, would still blindly obey, and once the work was finished would understand what he had not understood before and congratulate himself for having obeyed.

We would like to be able to tell of the thousand different impressions which the beauty of the Countess made on everyone depending on the different ways in which it manifested itself. At home, whimsically attired, while walking, laying indolently in her carriage or riding with inimitable elegance; at the theatre, with her divine hand resting on the velvet of the parapet, she was somewhat more attentive to the looks of admiration, directed from all sides and converging on her box, than to the music of Verdi or Meyerbeer... We would like, with that facility granted to writers of penetrating everywhere provided with the ring of Ariosto,[1] to lead the reader into the most intimate rooms and invite them to assist in the toilette of the Countess, who was a painting marked by antique Epicureanism, and reveal the secret treasures of that superhuman beauty, so very eager for admiration.

Her bedroom and other chambers were set apart from the rest of the apartments. Here, the exquisite taste of the great beauty showed itself more than anywhere else, that mark of the sovereign which she could not avoid laying on everything around her. Those rooms were a sanctuary. Everything that we can imagine by gathering together the easy comforts of our own modern habits and combining them with the majesty of antique decorations could be found there. The bedroom, in Pompeiian style, was full of exceedingly refined and extravagant paintings, extremely broad and bizarre friezes

---

1 Ludovico Ariosto, 1474-1533. In his *Orlando Furioso* there is a magic ring which makes the wearer invisible.

ran just below the base of the vaulted ceiling, which was itself covered with very delicate ornaments and chimerical figures; the furniture, the curtains, the draperies, everything agreed perfectly in style with the walls. The room was divided in two by a great arch, rich with carvings, decorations and very vague bas-reliefs, from which hung three silver lamps, antique and of the most pure and pretty design. An alcove closed off with curtains of soft, billowing silk contained the bed, which was covered with a layer of true purple, fringed with gold.

This room opened into a vast salon, also divided into two parts, the first of which served as a closet, the second as a bathroom. In the floor of the latter was sunk a large basin of green marble from which a fountain incessantly squirted, merrily pushing its spout toward the vault of the ceiling; along the sides were two porphyry baths and two big tables preciously sculpted, supporting the thousand objects necessary to a lady.

Through another door in the bedroom one entered into two small rooms, quite different and smaller. The first was extremely elegant.

From a rose-window in the middle of the ceiling velvet curtains, of that delicate pale pink which tinges the inside of some shells, descended and covered the whole room, vault and walls, falling down over a carpet, thick as the grass of a field, and also pink with white flowers. The sofa and the foot-stools were of this same velvet. The second room was even more curious, because turn where one might, nothing was seen but mirrors. Four chandeliers were placed in the corners. What frequently took place in those rooms was truly a scene that seemed to await the brush of some pagan artist. Sometimes the Countess, surrounded by her women, would spend a great deal of time dressing and arranging her hair, with a seriousness that reminded one of the Roman ladies, so if an indiscreet man were to have hidden himself behind a curtain he would have believed that he had been suddenly transported to the times of Juvenal;—yet another time, alone, she pleased herself voluptuously with the enchanting exhibition of her own beauty. She flung aside the fabrics and veils which were covering her and appeared, her own eyes dazzled by such perfection, beautiful as Venus rising from the sea.[1]—Then it almost seemed as if a mysterious trembling agitated the curtains, that the painted figures smiled, that the mirrors felt the image they were reflecting, as if that sculptural form gave involuntarily life to inanimate things.

If we were born during the time of Aspasia[2] or Phryne! Then we would have been allowed to describe minutely that body created effortlessly in a supreme moment of celestial inspiration—while instead our position as modern writer enjoins us to renounce telling of those elegant curves, those perfect lines, those harmonious forms which were like music descending from the sky; and it would be almost unallowable to sing one by one the stanzas of the poem of her body. Thus, we cannot even talk about the supreme line of the torso, nor about the arms which would have been given to the Venus de Milo; nor about the foot sim-

1 The celebrated Greek painter Apelles painted a picture of Venus rising from the sea, using the famous courtesan Phryne, who was widely considered to be the most beautiful woman in existence, as his model.
2 A notorious courtesan, the mistress of Pericles.

ilar to that of a goddess who has only touched the height of the clouds, nor about the leg of a rare purity of outline… and we are forced to leave the reader to make up for all of this with their own imagination, and in the place of our heroine put their own ideal.

Little by little her old habits regained their ascendancy, that *idée fixe* of her first years seized hold of her, yet with possibly more strength than before. By getting married, she was forced (as we have seen) to live a little the same life as everyone else, and this distracted her somewhat. Now she reverted; and in this there is certainly nothing amazing, because it was not possible that the occupations of society would suffice her, and of what could she have occupied herself with but herself, she who did not know love? Her husband, who at first suffered terribly from the fascination that she exercised on everyone, for the most part recovered from his passion, confronted as he was by her passive coldness.

She was bored by everything and, after her first year of marriage, retired for a long while before again appearing in society. The fact that lamentations arose from all sides at this disappearance and everyone was astonished can be easily understood. Yet, within herself, that *idée fixe* became almost an illness. When she was around twenty-five years of age, her beauty reached its culminating point and took the character of complete maturity. She was now the most perfect expression of womanhood and absolutely splendid in all her parts. The numerous mass of those who admired or secretly adored her—having well understood that this was a thing useless to speak of—now suffered because they were deprived of the joy of even seeing her. The very few who were granted a relative intimacy tried in every way to persuade her to seek some form of distraction. The artists, who studied her, understood that now the passion she had for her own self was prodigiously increasing.

Her husband, though unable to understand her, still saw with fearful astonishment the very strange light which burned more vividly in her eyes each day, and joined his prayers with theirs, but for some time everything was in vain.

Finally, one day, with a decision that seemed a mixture of her own will and a concession to the repetitive prayers, she consented to open her rooms for a great ball. The evening was fixed and the invitations descended amidst the thousands of conversations which were held concerning her desire of solitude, everybody pleasantly amazed.

The much anticipated evening came about. The carriages arrived in a long line and poured out their contingent of ladies and girls who slowly ascended a staircase covered with flowers. Snow-white mantles wrapped up and hid many beauties which in a moment were to be caressed by the brilliant light of the rooms. The magnificent apartments, quite brightly lit, all adorned with flowers, were filling up little by little. The Count, standing in the first room, received everyone with a stereotypical smile.

The dances had already begun when the Countess appeared, nothing about her person conforming to the commonplace. The effect that she produced was indescribable. There was a silence in the rooms as if a queen had arrived.

Her dress—of simple workmanship—was of red velvet and hung down, wrapping around her hips and extending behind her in an interminable train. On her bosom lay a very valuable emerald necklace. Her hair, of a colour between blonde and chestnut, had luminous and tawny reflections which begged for the brush of Titian and broke into masses of waves and curls, writhed in fantastic little spirals, and seemed as if alight with golden flames. Her skin was extremely white, but with a pallor that was lively and pink. Her eyes, of a very pure cut and calm splendour, were lethal without wanting to be. In her stately walk there was something divine; the rhythm of her voice blended with the rhythm of her movements.

Never before had she produced such a grand impression. Her beauty had acquired something luminous and fatal. She radiated and disturbed at the same time. Everyone was enraptured by her; and a few felt a pang in their hearts.

An old German scientist, talking to a friend by his side, said, while the Countess was passing:

"It is very strange to think that one day all this beauty will disappear, and that superb figure and those brilliant eyes will no longer claim more victims!"

Even though they were pronounced in an undertone, these words reached the ears of the Countess. She turned and replied with a smile and an inexplicable expression:

"No, doctor, you are mistaken. As long as I am, I will be as you see me now."

Throughout the evening she seemed very distracted. Her words were sometimes a bit incoherent and now and again a smile full of mysterious poetry passed over her lips.

The ball was magnificent. It was one of those entertainments that make history and remain as a model for all others, often for a very long time, like an inaccessible apex of richness and of elegance.

Since the beginning of the evening the Countess had not looked at herself. She seemed afraid. She enjoyed the admiration of others and wanted to wait for the assurance of her own. Meanwhile she relished her triumph, and the pride that filled her was so sweet that it was actually almost hard to bear. At about two o'clock, just when supper was being served and the rooms had emptied somewhat, she came to a sudden decision and made her way towards a sort of conservatory which was beside the ballroom, at the bottom of which stood an enormous mirror. She approached slowly with lowered eyes. It seemed as if she did not dare; but finally she raised her eyes.

It was as if a light spread over her face and her whole figure became illuminated. She remained motionless for a few minutes, absorbed, spellbound, with a smile of ecstatic satisfaction. Then, suddenly, she turned around and, walking with resolute steps through the groups of people who looked at her with some slight astonished, went towards her rooms.

She reached the room of mirrors.

There, with a rapid movement, she released her mass of hair and it fell loose in bright waves over her extremely white shoulders; she pulled away the hooks of her dress and it dropped to the floor; she shook away every veil and looked around. Joining her arms over her head she stood upright, with feet together and one hip slightly protruding, in a posture reminiscent of

Phryne in front of the Areopagus[1], and contemplating herself, she smiled.

Suddenly, she trembled with agitation—she became as pale as the marble statue of Pygmalion which, as soon as it had become a woman, turned into a statue again, then slowly crouched to the ground, like someone who feels they are losing their strength little by little. She fell to her knees, in the midst of her dresses and, bending slowly backwards, crossed her arms over her bosom and pulled whatever she could over herself with a gesture of extreme modesty.

That ball, which the Countess left before it ended, was for a long time the principle subject of conversation amongst elegant soci-

---

1 The Areopagus was a hill west of the Acropolis, in Athens, Greece. A judiciary council met there, which was also referred to as "the Areopagus." Phryne, after impersonating the goddess Aphrodite during a public festival, was brought before this council on charges of impiety, which was a capital offence. Her lawyer, Hypereides, tore away her clothing and the council, seeing her naked body, acquitted her, concurring that such divine beauty could not be an insult to the gods.

ety. It was also the last time that she showed herself in public.—Not long afterwards, she faded away.—Nobody surely has forgotten her death, as nobody has forgotten her beauty. She died after a brief and violent illness, which the doctors confessed they had not fully understood. Her body was embalmed. Her end was as mysterious as her life had been.

She remained an enigma to everyone. Certainly the image of a woman so beautiful, so seductive and insensitive, but completely possessed by an arcane passion, who passed by like an apparition—an object of amazement and desire—and then suddenly disappeared, will remain impressed in the memory of those who knew her for a very long time.

One day a group of friends were speaking of her. There was one who was enraptured by her beauty, which will remain as an inimitable type, and one who tried to explain the problem of her life. Then they began to discuss her death, which was still quite inexplicable.

"I know the reason," said a poet. "She died of beauty."

A Bet

THE following is what my friend was able to tell me about Count Sotowski, whose strange sadness had greatly excited my curiosity:

I have known him for many years and, having always found him to be amusing, jolly, and lively, was as surprised as you and everyone else at the change that came over him. The thing was, in fact, incomprehensible. As you know, he is fabulously rich, completely independent, with a graceful figure, a cheerful nature, and is extremely fortunate in his every endeavor; he was never known as one of those odd fellows who are able, with their imaginations, to create ghosts; he is continuously flattered by everyone, and has a great many friends who would do anything for him. How can one explain, then, the fact that previously he was energetic, serene, bright, so to speak, and that suddenly, without any obvious or evident reason he became the victim of a sombre melancholy?

It had been several months since I had seen him, when, running into him in Nice, I became aware of his strange melancholy. I didn't ask him the reason for it, as I knew it would be absolutely useless, since he is one of those fellows who only speak when they wish to. But I couldn't stop thinking about it and I racked my brain to discover the cause. You know how much psychological studies interest me, so you can easily understand.

Naturally, the first thing that came to mind was that he was suffering from a secret passion. What other cause could there be that would make a man with such a cheerful aspect and privy to such good fortune fall into melancholy if not the eternal source of tears down here—love?—The idea of a crime, of guilt, could not be admitted for a hundred reasons. But my imagination went flying over the range of possibilities and each day a new image of a heroine for my romance would appear. At times I thought that he might have loved a girl who, killed by a slow illness, had died in his arms; or maybe that he had been betrayed by some seductress, some *femme fatale*.

How mistaken I was!—One evening when we were together, far away from the fashionable promenade, in the area around the Pont du Var, and he looked more preoccupied than usual, he suddenly told me the reason for his sadness, without me having to ask or even expecting it. There was not a living soul along the long stretch of road; the sun was getting ready to descend into the sea, covering the clear sky with gold and purple; the air was becoming less suffocating than it had been during the day; and the Count's words sounded strange in the middle of that solitude and in the silence of the natural surroundings that would soon be asleep:

"I have something to confess," he said, "something which I have already noticed you are aware of—a sadness which, for some time now, has been afflicting me, and which I cannot drive away. I realize that when those who have known me for some time see this, they must be quite astonished; fortune has loaded me with its gifts and, moreover, I was born with an easy and cheerful personality. I have always been light-hearted, lively. I have never had sorrows or created them. Love's misfortunes are unknown to me."

"Really?" I replied. "Instead, when thinking of your melancholy, I immediately blamed it on an unhappy passion, not knowing what other misfortune you could possibly have been struck by."

"The fact is that I never met my father and the only sadness I can remember was the loss of my mother, but I was only ten years old and at that age one doesn't feel a great deal and easily forgets. After that, not a single cloud came across the horizon of my life. Everything smiled at me all the time; people and things.—But a terrible pain which I caused someone, which wasn't exactly my fault, and which, due to an extravagant and futile cause, has filled my soul with a bitterness which, I fear, will leave in me a great scar. It is a rather strange story."

"Tell me; you cannot imagine how interested I am."

He remained silent for a moment, as if absorbed in his thoughts, then asked:

"Have you ever heard the name Arnoldo D——?"

"I believe so," I replied. "He is a writer, if I am not mistaken."

"He was, you should say."

"He's dead?" I asked.

"No, but he has given up writing. He was a young man of an extraordinary intelligence, and certainly won't be forgotten by those who have read the few things he wrote. However, due to his rather irregular lifestyle, many found him disagreeable; he was poor, unlucky, with a lively and variable nature, often trying to drown his boredom in drunkenness or searching for some ever-more-crazy source of inspiration.

"He was born to be rich, but poverty, like an inauspicious ghost, would often approach him! He loved beautiful things, lavish rooms, the light of chandeliers and gems, soft carpets, Oriental luxury; he would have loved to have all those things, but only possessed them in his dreams, procured through fantasy or wine. His genius was not the sort that could flourish anywhere; in order to expand, it needed to be surrounded by wealth, by opulence. So, when he made some money, he would live like a prince for a month, then he would close himself off and work, and certainly with success; but finding himself once again broke, he would fall into dejection, inspiration would leave him and he was capable of nothing more than drinking to befuddle himself. He used to say that if he had had an income of one hundred thousand liras he would have been the greatest poet in the world.

"All these details were told to me later. I didn't know anything of this when we first met. I'm talking about many years before. From Italy, I had taken a trip to Paris and was then returning to Italy. We were on the Cenisio coach; it was night and I was peacefully sleeping in my corner seat of the *coupé*. Only one of the two other seats was taken, that in the opposite corner, of course, by a man huddled up, completely wrapped in his mantle, so that only his eyes could be seen.

"Waking from time to time, I had observed that he did not sleep, but it was not possible for me to see his face. At the break of day, he let fall the mantle and, the first light of dawn illuminating his pale features, I recognized Arnoldo D——, to whom I had never been introduced, but had seen many times here and there and whose writings I was familiar with.

"I was the first to speak, saying that I knew of him, and stating my name, and he, although a bit reluctant at first, soon started to talk with ease and at times with spirit. His conversation was entertaining to the highest degree; he had a decidedly original way of explaining things and I soon felt a strong liking for him, while at the same time I realized that I did not displease him, because at every moment he became more and more lively, opening up with ever-greater familiarity.

"After a few hours, we were almost friends. He told me about his projects, his aspirations, his troubles. He confessed that he did not know how to put up with poverty which, while spurring others on to work, to him was the biggest hindrance to the development of his genius. My name was not unknown to him and he was aware of my colossal fortune. He told me that if he had only had but a twentieth part of it, he would write a book that would not soon be forgotten and that would make him independently wealthy.

"We talked at length about art. The esteem for his genius that I had gained through reading his works increased even more, and I became convinced that he was a young man who would become famous if he did not lose himself in bad habits. Unfortunately, however, this was the road along which he was cynically advancing. His face already showed the signs, even though his features were quite handsome and his eyes thoughtful and shining;—even his conversation suffered somewhat, because at times he would wander into all sorts of puerilities or would let out curses and profanities without purpose. Despite this, it was a very pleasant day for me, and the hours spent on the coach, usually so boring, instead passed by quickly.

"I have always admired genius, in whatever form it manifests itself, and the works of others' imagination have always powerfully excited my own.—He was happy, one could see it, to have met someone who could truly understand him, and he talked about his private matters with a freedom that might have even astonished himself.

"The familiarity that came about spontaneously between two people who, by nature, were anything but exuberant must certainly have been caused by a secret and almost magnetic attraction. While speaking, he became increasingly more friendly, and I listened to him with ever-growing interest until, breaking with my usual reserve, I confessed to him all the admiration that his works had aroused in me, and how much I hoped that he would acquire an eternal position in the history of art.

"His eyes sparkled with enthusiasm when I spoke these words of encouragement. He became even more excited and recited a few verses which were well-rounded, harmonious, powerful. He then told me about his projects; he expounded the plot of a novel he was planning to write which to me seemed to abound in original effects and I exhorted him to begin with it as soon as he could. While talking about different things, he also told me of his particular liking for uncommon, extravagant, Hoffmanesque themes. Among his many ideas, he told me of one that he had not yet attempted to put to paper, and that he might never attempt, because it was far too difficult, although it had been running through his mind for a great while. It was, in fact, so very strange and uncommonly difficult, because all of its beauty would consist in the manner in which it would be written and because, in order for it to succeed, he would have to become embodied in the protagonist. It was, however, beautiful; and I had no doubt that if Arnoldo were to ever manage to write it, it would be a minor masterpiece. The subject appealed to me a great deal, and its fantastic originality interested me so much that I remained silent, turning it over in my mind. Its strangeness was almost doubled due to the extreme difficulty it would take to pull off.

"For a long while, neither of us spoke a word, both immersed in the same thought. The first the break the silence was Arnoldo:

"'It is one of those plots,' he said, 'that cannot be developed in a moment of inspiration. It is completely useless to plan to begin at a certain time and finish at another; one needs, on a certain day, which most certainly is not of one's choosing, to suddenly find oneself identifying with the protagonist, talking and acting in the same manner as he would have talked and acted in that circumstance. It's necessary, for a moment, to become him, and then, adopting his expressions, keeping his gestures, his comportment, his character, to talk and act so much like him as to give the story, despite its idealism, an imprint of undeniable truth. The poet, in this situation, is truly a slave of the moment, only taking action when the time is right, prepared to give up if his mind is still rebellious. And as much as it might give me pleasure, it would be useless to try to write it little by little, because it needs to come out all at once, and patiently I must await the day, which might be far in the future, when I shall pick up the pen and write, without stopping and without making corrections…'

"He said many such things, adding that the height of art is when it is not only the artist who does the work, but also when he is touched by a superhuman particle of fire that gives him the power to take the ephemeral and faded ideas which are outlined vaguely in the mist of his imagination and make them real. He explained all these things with true eloquence and profound conviction.

"One of his defects, however, was that he laughed a bit at everything; after his lips had twisted severely, he would suddenly display a cynical, mocking smile and with great spirit, compensated by eloquence, would argue the exact opposite of whatever point he had just made.

"He did just this regarding the situation of which we were then speaking. The echo, so to speak, of the fiery words he had used to excite my mind and compel me to think had not yet ceased, when he would start to say the very opposite. He reversed all his arguments, ridiculed his own ideas and was almost able to prove that all art was just a mechanism, that everything could be done with a number of specific components and that, with a bit of will power, any moment would be the right one. He now, in the same way he had previously been enthusiastic, discovered intonations so cynically correct that it was hard for me to fight against his irony, despite the fact that I had the same weapons as him. But he managed to draw me into an animated discussion before all of a sudden saying, as if to conclude:

"'After all, leaving theory aside, I could explain to you with an example the truth I am sustaining now against my false enthusiasm of a little while ago—and I'm certain you won't know how to respond.'

"'Fine, tell me then,' I replied, rather curious to hear what the devil he would come up with.

"'It's a very easy example to understand,' he continued. 'You'll agree with me, I hope, that the exceptional subject of the tale I told you about just now is fairly difficult, since, if I managed to prove to you that it could be done at any time, provided the right circumstances were in place, you would declare yourself persuaded that inspiration is not an essential element. But you will have to be satisfied with believing my words and trusting my conviction, because you certainly don't want to try it yourself. Listen: it has been a long time, as I've told you, that this subject has been occupying me and I have never been able to put it into deed; I am almost certain that the moment of inspiration will never come, because I will never be able to enter into the strange personality of my hero. Anyhow, I'm now tired from the trip, exhausted, sleepy…"

"'And so you would write it?' I interrupted, astonished.

"'I don't think,' he replied, 'that, with the lack of desire I feel and in this moment which is so little adapted to the task, I would be able to do so simply by an effort of the will. I would need stimulation, but you understand that if I could do it due to a non-artistic stimulation it would prove that the sacred fire is unnecessary. Well, if somebody were to tell me: "tomorrow morning you will be rich, if, during the night, you write the novel,"—my God! I would bet I could do it!'

"I was charmed by the originality of my new friend. A crazy idea rapidly crossed my mind; many such, however, were coming at that time. I said: 'What sum would you like?'

"'A sum that I certainly would not find any necromancer willing to give me. Five hundred thousand francs, for example.'

"'You will have them tomorrow morning if the story has been written.'

"Arnaldo could not believe it. He told me I was joking. I took a briefcase which contained everything I needed to write and clearly composed my pledge, then signed it with all my names and gave him the document. I told him:

"'Rest assured that I will not regret what I am now doing. If you lose, it will be the strongest proof against all those who don't believe in inspiration; if you win, I will have the pleasure of having contributed to your future, because your genius, as you yourself said, will gain fresh momentum and you will never seek courage in——'

"'You're right!' he interrupted. 'You could never imagine the good you are doing at this moment and how grateful I shall be! May the Muses bless you!'

"He was unable to moderate his joy; he sang, laughed, said all sorts of nonsense. He was absolutely sure he would succeed. Madly he talked about what he would do once rich; he said he was now finally sure that he would really make a name for himself. I was happy to see him so cheerful due to me; I was gloating in my turn (I must confess) at having done something that certainly isn't done every day. I thought, if he won, and once the elation of the moment had passed, that perhaps I would be annoyed at having given such a large sum to somebody who in the end I knew only by name; but on the other hand, it seemed to me not unlikely that he would fail, despite his confidence.

"We got to Turin at around eleven o'clock, and as soon as we entered the hotel he ordered his supper and asked for it to be brought to his room. We shook hands and he said to me:

"'I'm off to work. You shall have your story tomorrow.'

"Being quite tired, I slept deeply throughout the night, and woke up around nine.

"I immediately ran to Arnoldo's room and found the door wide open. Nobody was within. I went downstairs and asked the hotelier about the gentleman who I had arrived with.

"'He left about an hour ago.'

"'What? He's left?'

"'Yes, signore. In fact… I wouldn't wish to worry you, but it seems to me that something must have happened to that gentleman.'

"'And why is that?' I asked, even though I was beginning to suspect the truth.

"'As you know, your friend had dinner brought up to his room when you arrived last night; the attendant lit two candles and asked him if he needed anything else, to which he replied: "Nothing!" and so the attendant left. Well, the latter stayed up most of the night and the light still shone in your friend's window. The other attendant, who woke up at five, when the first went to bed, saw the light still shining. Finally, at around eight, the gentleman rang the bell, and the attendant, entering the room, found him sitting at the table, with paper in front of him, the two candles almost expired, and (by this he was quite struck) as pale as a dead man.'

"'And what did he say?'

"'He was of a frightening pallor and his voice corresponded to his face, as it was shaky and somewhat hoarse. He asked at what time the first train left, told him to take down his suitcase, and, wrapped in a cloak, came and sat in this chair to wait until the horses were hitched to the omnibus. I was at that table, writing, and pretending not to take any notice of him, though I observed him stealthily, and saw him strike his forehead two or three times and in a low voice utter strange words. I dared not ask him anything, since he seemed in such a bad humour that he certainly would not have welcomed my inquiry.'

"'And he left?'

"'Yes, signore. He got into the omnibus, giving, in an off-hand manner, a generous tip to the attendant, and was taken to the station where he took the train to Genoa, which was the first to leave.'

"All these details remain etched in my memory. I asked if he had left anything for me and I was told that he hadn't.

"A horrible suspicion suddenly took hold of me and I understood how imprudent my pledge had been. It was clear that he had not been able to write the story, and with the ease in which he was able to fall into extreme moods and to abandon himself to the impressions of the moment, he had plunged into desperation. With that habitually strange imagination, and agitated by a disillusionment so forceful, anything was possible; a shiver of indescribable fear ran through my bones. I was determined to find him.

"My search was fruitless. Neither in Genoa or elsewhere could I find a trace of Arnoldo D——. I looked everywhere: hotels, houses, cafés, theatres, taverns. I bothered at least a hundred people with my questions, without anyone being able to tell me anything precise. He certainly had not stopped in Genoa. I went back to Turin, and then on to Milan, searching again, and always, uselessly. I knew that he had family in Venice; and there I went. Fifteen days had already gone by.

"In Venice I was finally informed of the sad truth. Although I always repelled it, the idea of suicide had come to my mind many times. The truth was perhaps worse: he had gone mad!"

The count stopped and took a few steps in silence, absorbed in his thoughts. I did not dare disturb him and waited until he continued, this time in a low and sad voice:

"Now you can understand the reason for the melancholy by which I am pursued, always and everywhere. It is a blend of sadness and remorse. Due to a bizarre, prodigal idea I have probably suppressed an uncommon genius and cast into the gloom a soul that was shining in the light. In order to console myself I can say that I could not have foreseen such a catastrophe and that he was already, by nature, so odd that all the blame cannot be assigned to the failed test; but for me these excuses do not suffice. So profound was his dejection, his anger, his distress at not being able to do that which he had been sure of and that which would have guaranteed him wealth—his life's dream—that all the hallucinations of his mind, his eccentricities, the consequences of his vice, took hold of him and his reason vanished. I tried to see him but was only able to two months after the fatal day; nothing, however, could relieve him of his madness. He is habitually sad, downcast, sometimes furious; his words always refer to that night during which he worked while I slept, unaware of the evil that that unsuccessful effort would have on his diseased mind."

It was night when we reached Sotowski's house. The moon, reflected in an ocean as calm as if it were asleep, created a long strip of diamond-studded light which seemed like a path of visions; the stars sparkled. I told him that I now understood everything, thanked him and shook his hand, and, due to the outpouring he had had, he seemed less agitated than usual. Now we knew the reason for the Count's profound sorrow; though strange, anyone who has experienced remorse for having done a great moral evil, even involuntarily, would sympathize.

I saw the Count many more times, but he did not return to this scabrous subject, and I did not dare to invoke it. One evening, however, many after that which I have spoken of, he told me that he could give me the conclusion to the curious anecdote that he had narrated.

"That evening, when I was leaving D——,
I had told him that I would be going to
Florence, and he, two days later, before being
struck by his misfortune, sent a letter to me
there, which I did not read until twenty days
later, when he had already been seized by madness and I knew this sad truth. Read it, as you
might find it interesting; but let us not speak
of the matter again."

I obeyed and the following day, without an
additional word, returned the letter to him;
but truly, I had found it interesting.

> To Count Sigismondo Sotowski
> Genoa.....

> It is impossible for me to see
> you again—I cannot! Thus I
> write you these lines that I am
> sending to Florence where you
> will soon be going, according to
> your plans.—Aeschylus, Homer,
> Dante, Shakespeare and the rest,
> can you see them shining brightly

in the sky of the past, surrounded by unchanging eternal light? The seats have already been taken, no one else can join that group. It has been said: "Where there is a will, there is a way."

This is false. I was unable to be rich—I who have always wished for it, who would have had genius if I had had gold, who would have found happiness if I had written the story. I did not know how to do it.

Count, do not imagine that inspiration is necessary; it is simply that the devil put his tail in it. If you could only imagine what the anger was like at first! Now that I am much calmer, I feel light, stupid and peaceful. From my window I see the harbour and it seems to me that there are few earthly pleasures greater than counting the masts of the ships; but it is quite difficult, as each one hides the next. It seems strange that several days have already passed: my ideas are much clearer than normal, but sometimes I cry and then laugh for no precise reason. So that evening I went into the hotel room, determined to work and sure that I would succeed. I was happy and full of joy; a dream of mine had come true. Yes, sir, I must confess to you that I had dreamed of the enterprise you proposed to me many times. When I would exclaim: "If I were a millionaire I would be a great poet!" I would often add: "If someone were to tell me, 'Write something that will endure, and tomorrow morning you will be rich,' I don't know what I would not be able to do!"—I sat at the table and began to think. Have you ever had that strange sensation when thoughts deviate of their own accord? when, rebellious, they go wherever they wish? That is how I felt at that moment. My imagination, instead of applying itself to the protagonist of the story, in whose person I needed to enter, made pass before my eyes the five hundred thousand things I would be able to do the next day with five hundred thousand francs, meanwhile forgetting to earn them. I had thought that my genius would blossom, that I would write a book that would make my fortune and in a few years my capital would triple. I thought that finally each of my repressed desires would be able to be satisfied, that those things longed for in vain could be mine: that the velvet and the satin, the Persian carpets and Oriental pearls, the dinners, voyages and romances would be mine; that all the beautiful, fine and pleasant things that until then had seemed to me to be the exclusive earthly birthright of imbeciles, would be mine; that I would now be able to travel on a special train like a monarch and have my poems printed on silver paper in letters of gold! I dreamed of the pleasure, success, enjoyment that the future had prepared for me as compensation for past miseries; it seemed to me that paradise had suddenly become a terrestrial thing—it seemed that I was above everything, and I was stirred by an immense pride, thinking that I would soon be able to take revenge for all the humiliations I had received; I saw that, before not very long, I would be richer than the Rothschilds, lord of satisfying my own prodigality, which would be divided into two streams, one of gold and another of words—of diamonds and of poetry!

In this manner I heard one o'clock strike. I wrote a few lines. I mused. It seemed to me that only a few minutes had gone by when two strokes were heard from the clock.

A shiver ran through my entire body. It seemed as if time was escaping from me like something slipping from between my hands. I looked with terror at the sheets of white paper before me. I dipped my pen in the ink to continue, but words would not come. Also, I reflected that before writing it was necessary for me to enter into the spirit of the subject, to think as would the protagonist. I made a violent effort and forced my mind to go within those bounds; but it would sometimes stray and I was not able to comprehend how long that straying lasted.

Three o'clock struck. I understood that I needed to do

something, to be strong. Above all it was necessary to think well first and not to write over-hastily, otherwise the time would pass in failed attempts and my mind would become confused in feverish efforts. I got up and began to pace back and forth, trying to gather my thoughts together to the one place they needed to be.

Another hour passed in this manner, and the clock above the fireplace struck four. Then my composure left me again and I was overcome by a horrible fear. It was necessary to write. That paper, obstinately white in front of me, made me angry. Resolutely I began, however I might, simply to begin. I had only written a few lines, but already began to feel a variety of relief... I remained motionless for a moment, not thinking of anything. Then I wanted to continue; I began to think again… and I thought for such a long time that five notes sounded from the clock.

Cold drops of sweat moistened my forehead. It seemed as if those accursed blows were vibrating the hour of my doom. A kind of nervous tremor assailed me; I bit my hand with violence. I stood up and again stalked the length and breadth of the room like a wild beast in a cage, which relieved me somewhat. A bit calmer, I sat back down—but now the plans of what I would do with my wealth and the thoughts about my protagonist swarmed confusedly together in my brain. Time passed, fear growing stronger every moment and, beginning to understand that I was losing everything, I made a supreme effort and wrote an entire page. Hope returned slowly to my heart and I felt somewhat reassured.

Yet, as I wrote, every minute the thought came back to me ever more vigorously and frightening that time was flying, that the work was far from completion, that I would not be able to complete it. My pen sped quickly, anxiously over the paper; my hand was trembling...

Suddenly I realized that a faint, pale ray of dawn was penetrating through the half-closed shutters and was striking against my distraught face together with the dim light of the candles. All was finished. I attempted to shake myself, prayed and cursed at the same time. I reread what I had written: the last lines were without meaning.

I was overcome with despair. I had lost! My hand was trembling so much that I would not even have been able to hold the pen.

A few days later after having written this letter, he completely lost his mind.

"But, for pity's sake, don't tell Sotowski that I told you his story, because he wants to keep it a secret," my friend concluded.

A SONG BY WEBER

I.

IT was an old house full of memories; large, brown, and regular, covered here and there by the severe green of ivy. It was situated on a small rise and was reached by means of a long avenue, gloomy and aristocratic, flanked on both sides by hundred-year-old trees. At the end of it one could see a great iron gate, rusted by time, which would creak ruefully every time it was made to turn on its badly connected hinges. Compared to the old feudal castle, the superb ruins of which could be seen on a distant hill, the house of which we speak seemed new; but if it were compared instead to the white cottages and the modern little church of the village below, it would withal inspire profound respect. And although it had not, like the castle up over there, seen unfold between its walls tenebrous medieval dramas, and seen pass at its feet iron-clad knights, it had, all the same, witnessed a great many things. Built towards the end of the reign of Louis XIV, it had had in its salons the magnificent entertainments of that time, with marquises wearing enormous curly wigs, and beautiful ladies with painted faces and eyes sparkling with promises... completely covered in satin and gems, with puffed up skirts and pride. Later it had witnessed the orgies of the Regency, brought in from Paris to the *vie de Château,* and it recalled the powder and the red heels of the gentlemen and the effeminate white hands of the little amorous abbots.

The terrible wind of the revolution had blown over its roof without demolishing it; the wars of the Empire had respected it. After the dinners of the Regency it had witnessed the carousals of the Directorate; within its walls voices cursing Bonaparte had been heard (in the way the supporters of the old state of things referred to the emperor), and now, in the first half of this century it stood still strong and proud in its place, although a bit run down due to the indifference of its owners.

It belonged to the Counts of Montsauron, an important family already illustrious at the time of the Crusades. But of that long lineage, with its coat of arms completely covered with quarterings, who now remained?—an old man, a living relic of a time gone by, who, through the shocks of the revolution and the victories of the emperor, had preserved his ideas in full, his possessions in part, the powder in his hair, and the golden buckles on his shoes. He was a man who did not lack intelligence, but obstinately clung to his prejudices, like ivy to a ruin, full of arrogance and the already stale spirit of his time.

Though still rich despite political vicissitudes, he was not able to keep his house in the same splendor as before; so now weeds grew from between the broken stones of the court of honour, and the terraces and richly decorated balustrades were all green from humidity. The living parasites had ended their reign inside the house that had grown so quiet by now, but in exchange, parasitic vegetation climbed in disorder on the walls outside with a freedom that was truly revolutionary.—The great salons were naked, cold and stern. Those chairs with the uncomfortable and unpleasant style that was used under the Empire, those tables covered with chilly marble, white or veined, with little legs adorned at the top with gilded snapdragons and tapering towards their base, those sofas, so straight and hard, with cushions attached to the wooden arms with ribbons, gave a rather disheartening impression and had little to do with modern customs. The transoms, in a Pompadour style, had nothing to do with the rest.—In the gardens the shrubs, which had been trimmed in regular designs and shapes according to the fashion of the time, had regained complete wild freedom and extended their branches with the most disobedient license.

And the old gentleman lived there alone with his daughter, a young lady of around twenty, beautiful, tall, with a graceful figure, a dainty expression, and very delicate features. She had magnificent light brown hair which under bright light took on reflections impossible to describe, and two big blue eyes, thoughtful and passionate, that looked at one as very few eyes look.

And, apart from the village priest, now and again some family from the area, and the old servants—who believed themselves to be part of the house and wore their threadbare green and gold livery with the same pride as their master wore his court dress—he did not see anyone and lived alone with his Ida, whose youth was like a ray of sunshine shining through the old house.

The servants still remembered the time when their master lived in Paris, among the many entertainments of society, and would not leave that wonderful sojourn but for a few months, which, however, were invariably passed in the old mansion. So it was that for eight months a year the vaulted roofs of the long salons were untouched by an echo, the shutters remained hermetically closed, and life was not resumed until autumn. When that season came about, one could see the dusty carriages proceeding along the gloomy avenue, coming from Paris, pulled by four vigorous horses mounted by postillions dressed in the Count's livery, who gaily flicked their whips.

Now, however, he no longer left the old house, living there four seasons in succession. He lunched, with his daughter, in a large room on the ground floor, served by five servants, who kept themselves quite busy doing nothing; and certainly such opulence in solitude would have seemed rather sad to many.

One fine day the Count received a letter with a large emblazoned seal. He hastily opened it and, reading the first lines, his eyes lit up with joy. He re-read the letter several times with obvious satisfaction and for the rest of the day was in an unusually good mood, as if ten years had been lifted from his shoulders. He walked with a brisk and buoyant step, chattered more than usual—smiling at everyone—at every moment kissing his daughter on the forehead and telling her that he had never seen her look so beautiful.

The following day his behavior became decidedly extravagant. It seemed as if his nature had changed. He, who in his own way was so fond of order, never wishing to have any item of furniture moved from one room to another—he, who was a declared foe of disarray, started to turn everything upside down, to do and redo, to rearrange everything he saw around him. It seemed as if he wanted to give a new look to the old house, despite him loving it so much as it was.

The large reception rooms, closed for many years, were opened; the cloth covers were taken off the furniture, the majestic pleats of the curtains carefully dusted, the cobwebs swept from the corners of the ceiling where they cosily hung, the veils removed from the mirrors, and the vases filled with flowers. The magnificent service in solid silver, a gift from a duke of Savoy to the house of Montsauron, was taken from an old cupboard where it had been kept in the dark for who knew how long. The servants flitted hastily about everywhere, quietly asking each other questions, very much surprised at the order they had received to clean to their utmost ability and to put on the livery for special occasions.

The mould that was on the terrace was scraped away. The garden was raked, the fallen leaves removed from the paths, the withered flowers plucked; branches that were too long were trimmed, and there was an attempt at giving back to some of the shrubs their original architectural shapes.

Something extraordinary was certainly going to happen.

Ida was not aware of all this. She never dared to bother her father when he did not come to her. So, that morning, not seeing him appear, she had already gone to her favourite place, a corner room at the end of the left wing of the house. It was there that her most intimate friend, the piano, was.

And here the very strong passion Ida had for music should be mentioned. Instinctively she knew how to play the harpsichord,—she sang because God had told her to sing.

The only teacher she had had, and quite late, was a young man who was under the protection of the Count, and who belonged to a family who had taken refuge in that quiet village after the Terror. His father, although poor and unknown, was a genuine artist—one of the many who pass by, radiant but unseen. He concentrated all his life's attention on the education of his son. The mother had died; the poor boy was but sixteen years old when his father passed away as well. He found himself alone, rich in only youth and hope. The Comte de Montsauron gave him his protection: he got a publisher in Paris to buy a few of his compositions, and tasked him with giving lessons to his daughter.—To many it might seem strange that a man with a mindset such as the old Count had would put a young fellow of twenty-five years near his daughter, but it should be understood that Paolo was serious and sober, and that Ida had seen him about for so long that she surely considered him to be part of the household furniture. Moreover, during that period in which the aristocracy still proudly supported all the caste prejudices, not even the slightest thought could have entered the Count's mind that his daughter could cast a single glance at a person as obscure as the poor musician. He also often sat in during the lessons.

Hence, Ida had opened the harpsichord and was letting her beautiful fingers wander over the keys, when the Count suddenly entered—something unusual at that hour. He was dressed with utmost care and his face seemed to be beaming with an expression of gladness. He came closer to his daughter, took her two hands in his and kissing her forehead said:

"I urge you, my dear, to pretty yourself up today—to make yourself as pretty as possible!"

And a smile full of meaning passed over his lips.

"Why, father?" Ida asked, staring at him with her big blue eyes.

"Why? You will find out soon enough."

"Maybe you are expecting someone?"

Another smile, more prolonged than the first, lit up the Count's face.

And in a few words he told his daughter, who was quite amazed at such an extraordinary occurrence, that he was actually waiting for someone, the Marquis di Sentis, a distant relative.

"The letter that you saw me reading came from him. He should arrive today. He is a handsome, pleasant and fine young man, a proper gentleman, and the owner of large properties in Normandy that those scoundrels of '93 were not able to snatch from him. The estate of Sentis Castle alone yields fifty thousand écus a year."

A few hours later the Marquis arrived. Ida saw that her father had told her the truth. He might have been between thirty-five and forty years old; tall, quite well made, with regular features, and a very distinguished face which indicated a man of high intelligence. He had excellent manners, a sympathetic tone of voice and was dressed with a sober elegance that stamped him as a man of taste from head to toe.

He arrived in a large Berlin carriage, which he swiftly descended from and climbed the steps to the terrace (where the old Count had come to meet him), with his hat in his hand and a smile on his lips. He replied warmly to the warm welcome that the lord of the place showed him, and then, turning towards Ida who was standing a little to one side, he kissed the tips of her fingers with such a respectful gallantry that it reminded her of Versailles, saying to her:

"My beautiful young lady, please allow your cousin to offer you his homage. I came prepared to admire your beauty and grace, but if I had known the reality that awaited me I would not have believed that it was possible to find such a thing without leaving the confines of the earth."

He then turned towards the Count, and dedicated himself entirely to him as if Ida was not present.

A little later they went to table, and throughout lunch the Marquis kept up a brilliant and flowery conversation, always being extremely cordial towards the father, and with the daughter showing a gallantry dated two centuries previous.

That night, Ida slept poorly. An event such as the arrival, so little expected, of that elegant cousin, was naturally going to occupy her imagination. Moreover, a secret voice, that she herself was unable to explain, was warning her that the Marquis di Sentis had come for her.

We have already said that Ida was almost twenty years old. Her beautiful youth shone on her forehead like a halo and sang in her heart like a siren. Yet she had lived so quietly. She knew little of the world; the busy life that her young peers led in the capital, that splendid circle of amusement and boredom, she knew only through words. Her heart beat, but it had never throbbed. The intoxicating breath of spring, which makes the roses seem more fragrant and the stars brighter, had wafted over her—but about love she was still ignorant. She had one of those natures which is passive and indifferent, though full of hidden passion—but of that she was ignorant. She had been given, by the standards of that period, a good education—in which the strictest religious principles were put foremost—and in her head the idea had been well lodged that the Montsauron were among the most important families in France, and that she was destined for a great marriage.

Her predictions regarding the Marquis were not incorrect. The following day, first thing in the morning, her father came into her room, kissed her even more affectionately than the day before, and sat down beside her, saying that he needed to talk to her about important things. In a few words he told her that the Marquis di Sentis had come from his estate in Normandy for the precise purpose of seeing her—because he wanted to get married and thought that a union with their house would be an honour—he found her more beautiful than he had expected and asked for her hand. He still had a few matters to attend to at Sentis Castle, but would soon be back to receive her answer.

"He has a great name and is quite agreeable. Yesterday it seemed to me that you were not displeased by him. My dear, I have no doubts about your reply."

All this Ida somewhat expected. Why then did her father's words have a strange effect on her? She felt a pang in her heart and the slight blush, that had appeared on her face at first, turned into pallor. Was it perhaps a premonition?

The Count, attributing that confusion to a completely different cause than the real one, added, smiling knowingly:

"You are not answering, my dear? Indeed, in such circumstances as this silence is the best reply." And so saying he quickly exited.

Ida, left alone, felt troubled. She sat down and thought.

She thought for a good quarter of an hour, her hands folded over each other, her eyes staring at the floor, her head lowered, her brow darkened.

What was she thinking about?—She herself did not really know; her thoughts ran on, ran on without her understanding where they were going.

Who knows for how long she would have stayed that way if she had not suddenly heard someone knocking on the door.

The maid came in, saying:

"The music teacher is in the green room and awaits mademoiselle."

We have already mentioned the green room, which is the room with the piano. Its name came from the green wallpaper, which was of a pale green, faded by time. It was not very large, but had a very high ceiling; though it did not have much in the way of decoration and was rather shabby, from the open window one could enjoy a splendid view and the whispering of the wind among the leaves of a chestnut tree, the branches of which stretched before it.

The pianoforte, the *clavecin*, as it was called at that time, stood in the centre. This too, like the rest of the furniture, was of the empire style, tall and thin, made from a light-colored wood, completely inlaid.

When Ida entered, Paolo was at the harpsichord playing a piece by Gluck, using the soft pedal. He stood up when she appeared, greeting her with an inflexion of voice that simultaneously demonstrated the familiarity derived from meeting often and the respect which she was due. Ida sat near him and the lesson began.

For nearly two years this had been happening two or three times a week.

Paolo had rarely been to Paris and he had never had, so to speak, the time to be young. He had been forced to stifle the great aspirations that came with his age. Since his early years, life had appeared to him to have a rather grave face, and the bitter struggle for necessities and the school of misfortune had left a mark of early maturity on his brow.

Is it then surprising that the frequent company of Ida had made such a deep impression on him?

To put it simply—although he had tried to fight against the sentiment that overwhelmed him, since it could only have sad consequences—in the end he still had to confess to himself that he loved her.

And truly he loved her so much that he did not dare to calmly examine his own soul; he was afraid of the dizziness and did not want to look into the abyss.

And Ida?

She still knew nothing about love, though her sensitive soul and, more than anything, her innate passion for music—which is the greatest translation of love that there is beneath heaven—would surely, at twenty years of age, affect her before long.

Though not a single frivolous word had been exchanged between those two, a bond still existed—harmony.

Many times, when the beautiful fingers of the young lady glided over the ivory keys of the old harpsichord, making it vibrate with the passionate accents of Italian music or sweet German melodies, her heart beat strangely and she dared not turn to look at her teacher, who stood motionless behind her chair, adoring her despite himself.

And when she sang and repeated the harmonies of the great masters, which in that moment seemed to be improvisations of her own soul—with those blue eyes in which an arcane light was kindled looking into space, as if she were having a vision of the sky suddenly opening—with her hair wafted by a breeze coming in from the large window—oh! at that moment the poor artist would have given his life to have been able to hold her in his arms, to feel that she was his!

He had been able to control himself and no words had come from his lips. She, on her part, was courteous with him, at times even friendly, but nothing more.

And so this time the lesson started as usual. Paolo was pale, of a pallor that was not normal for him.

He was suffering deeply. He had heard everything. The arrival of the Marquis had for him been a revelation and a thunderbolt. He had immediately understood why that man had come. And although his love for Ida was without the slightest hope—still, the announcement of the imminent marriage was like the cold blade of a dagger being thrust into his heart.

Once married, Ida would leave. The comfort, which *was* a comfort, of seeing her almost every day, of often sitting at her harpsichord, of listening to her beloved voice… was going to be cruelly taken from him. And knowing she belonged to somebody else!… He could not stop thinking of it. And then the torment, the torture of having to witness the joy of others, with a serene countenance and hell in his heart, of having to attend the wedding festival, and maybe even the ceremony!… And the fear of betraying himself!… Would he be able to keep silent until the last moment, to repress the beating of his heart and hold back the tears from his eyes? Would he have the pitiful strength to play his part properly to the end, to all that time keep wearing the mask he had put on?

Ida was also sad.—Suddenly she abandoned the piece she was playing and leaned on the music stand with her head in her hands. Paolo was silent.

After a few moments she raised her head and, instead of continuing the piece she had already begun, sang her favourite song.

It was a song by Weber—we do not know which one precisely—but one of those into which the great German composer had poured the entirety of his artist's soul. The motif arose simple, clear—a rueful, sad melody, full of sweet languors and heartrending accents, as enchanting as a love poem, as gloomy as the vanishing of a hope. Then it lit up, vivified, becoming as strong as the roar of a tempest, struggled as if it were a battle within the heart. Meanwhile the motif filtered through. Then it found itself once more alone and ended in a repeated and dying echo.

Ida had played it and sung it twenty times a day. And the way she did it!… In those moments she had been so beautiful that she almost no longer seemed to be an earthly creature. This time, with her soul involuntarily full of sadness, she sang those sublime notes with so much emotion that they seemed like her heart's supreme cry.

To Paolo, the notes of that song all sounded like an excruciating note of farewell. When the music had ceased, agitated and unable any longer to resist the anxiety to know the truth, the entire truth (even though he had promised himself not to utter a word on the subject), he said in a soft voice that he tried in vain to render calm:

"Mademoiselle, excuse my indiscretion... but I have a question to ask you."

"What question?"

"About something which concerns you very... very intimately."

"Say it, say it," Ida replied, becoming pale in spite of herself.

"Is it true that..."

The poor young man felt suffocated.

"That the Marquis di Sentis has asked for my hand?" Ida interrupted ardently. "Yes, it's true."

She said these words quickly, in a frank and confident tone… even though she was distraught. She got up and closed the harpsichord. She stood motionless and thoughtful for a moment, said that it was enough for that day, said goodbye to Paolo, who looked petrified, and left.

When Paolo found himself alone, he sat at Ida's place and buried his face in his hands.

Ida, on her part, had, due to Paolo's agitation, guessed everything. Through a sudden revelation, she had simultaneously betrayed love and understood that he loved her.

Meanwhile, the planned wedding did not give her much happiness. She felt a dislike for the Marquis which, though certainly unjustified, was invincible.

That evening, she told her father that she would not marry him.

But then the Count, on his part, started the slow work of persuasion. He cherished her in a way he had not for a long time. He showed her that by refusing his hand she was refusing her own happiness; he told her that she would certainly learn to love the Marquis; and, in short, all the reasons, good and bad, that he could find. He sang the Marquis' praises, listing his many qualities, enticed the young woman's imagination with images of the luxury and triumphs which awaited her in Paris. He spoke so much and so well that she finally gave in and gave her consent.

Ah, imprudent girl!… She did not know what she was doing. That heart which she let herself be persuaded to give to another was already no longer hers.

It was not long before she realized this.

In the evening she retired to her room early and found herself quite sad over the decision she had made. It seemed to her that it would be impossible to leave that house where she had been born, to abandon her father and her few old friends.

And poor Paolo?… "I will no longer sing that song by Weber with him, which I adore and which he loves to listen to so much!…" Thinking about all this, there in the nocturnal solitude of her virginal room, which she would soon have to leave, her heart suddenly swelled, she felt a sadness ignored until then, and she wept bitterly. O love!… You were there!

The next day, when she left her room, she found Paolo in the drawing room. Why had he come when normally he was only seen at the time set aside for the lesson?—He was pale and his dull gaze indicated a long night of insomnia.

Ida felt her heart beating against the silk of her dress.

The poor young lady was somewhat overwrought.

"Paolo," she said, "I consented."

It was the first time she had addressed him like that.

He understood that he could no longer resist.

"I consented," she repeated. "Today my father will write to the Marquis di Sentis, who will not delay in coming.—And in a month I will be his wife... and will have to leave this house... and my father, and friends...

She hid her pretty face in her handkerchief and wept again.

Paolo was pale and his lips trembled convulsively.

"Mademoiselle," he said at last, "and will you remember your friends from here now and again?…"

"Yes, always…" Ida murmured. "But now, goodbye."

So saying she stretched out her hand.

He took it; it was ice-cold. He squeezed it passionately.—And the levee was broken.

"You will go, mademoiselle, and I will remain; but only for a short while. I cannot live without you, and once you are the Marchioness di Sentis I shall die.—I had sworn to stay silent, but human strength has its limits. I love you, Ida. In this final hour, in this sorrowful hour of farewell, I am unsure how I might dare say it, but I will. I love you, I adore you, I only live for you. I know by how much we are separated. You would never have been able to have loved me. You have done well to accept the Marquis' hand.—Be happy, Ida… but think now and again that there is someone down here who would die with a smile on his lips if he could die for you…"

"Paolo, I too…"

At that moment the door opened and the Count entered the room. From the attitude of the two young people, he quickly intuited what was occurring. His brow furrowed.—Paolo, completely losing his head, fled.

Ida was overwrought.

"Father," she exclaimed, "I will never marry the Marquis di Sentis. Never! never! never!…"

"Actually though, you will marry him in a week," said the Count. His voice was firm, but quite tender.

He entered into a long discourse. He told her that he understood quite well that her sudden change was simply a girlish caprice for Paolo.—He showed her, affectionately and paternally, how one needed to contend with such a sentiment.—She would never have been able to marry him anyhow, so…?

He was kind, but inflexible.

For the second time Ida was almost won over by the words of her father. And when he left her, she seemed to have accepted things. She was, like the Count, imbued with the aristocratic ideas of the time. She knew that Paolo could not be her husband.—Why then not accept the Marquis' hand? Why bring so much displeasure to a father who adored her?—A change in life would make her forget much; the Marquis was an extremely amiable man, and then... She could see Paolo again sometimes... infrequently, like a friend... Ingenuously she thought thus.

And so it was that she gradually reconciled herself to the idea of marriage; and that evening, tired from the emotions of the day, she went to sleep early—somewhat sad, but calm.

The next day Paolo came at the usual time.

He had reflected for a good while on his position. He understood that if, at the moment of the marriage between Ida and the Marquis, he stood in the way, it would be showing a great deal of ingratitude towards the Count, to whom he owed so much, causing him much anguish, while at the same time obstructing Ida's future without gaining any advantage. He loved her madly, but swore to himself to be strong.

When he presented himself, he was pale and melancholy, but resigned. Ida told him that she had definitely consented. She exposed her naked soul; not knowing how to keep silent, she confessed her love with that sublime blindness of passion that does not exclude modesty, and at the same time she tried to share some of her fictitious strength with him. She told him to remember that she would never love anyone on earth but him,—but she added what he already knew too well: that this love was impossible. That she would always show him her affection and that she hoped—in a year—to see him at Sentis Castle.

"Never," he replied, "never could I see you as another's. You are right, mademoiselle; marry the Marquis, perhaps he will understand how to make you happy, and... forget me. I will no longer come for the lesson. The Count has told me that now you will be so busy in your preparations that you will no longer have time for music. He does well... it is much better that I do not see you. Before your departure..."—here his voice became emotional, but he continued—"I shall come back one last time to say goodbye..."

Ida felt like crying,—she could not speak. She stretched out her hand. He brought it to his lips, and left.

✳

Within a few days, with a strength of feeling that she had never experienced before, Ida's melancholy changed into a dark, gloomy, frightening sadness. A most bitter repentance for having consented abruptly took hold of her so violently that it seemed that remorse was preying on her conscience. Instead, love arose slowly and strongly in her, and filled her completely. She would have sacrificed everything to have been able to take back her consent, but she understood that she could no longer retreat, and as if taken by vertigo, she walked straight towards the precipice. If she had begged her father, he would have treated her entreaty as a whim… and who could tell?… perhaps he would have forced her. From day to day her sadness grew. She painfully admitted to herself that she would have now preferred the convent to the Marquis di Sentis; she felt, unfortunately, that she would never be but a hopeless victim.

The Marquis arrived. Neither his courtesy nor his impeccable gallantry were able to clear the cloud of sadness that weighed on the brow of the repentant young woman.

The Count persuaded himself that it was best to hasten matters, and the marriage was arranged for the following Sunday. The guests arrived from Paris. They were the Count's few relatives, and numerous friends of the Marquis di Sentis. The old house, calm and quiet, was, for a moment, full of the noise and liveliness that had stirred it in times gone by. The Count entertained his guests splendidly.—There were days of continuous celebration. Amidst all of that hubbub Ida ended up distracting herself a bit.

However, when she woke up on Saturday morning, the horror of her position appeared enormous. "It's tomorrow," she thought. "Tomorrow all will be finished."

Paolo had never come to see her again. She dared not think of his promise to return to say goodbye... On the contrary, she tried to drive the thought away... but the thought returned.

She went to the room where the harpsichord was and began to sing her favourite song. It had now acquired a new fascination in her eyes; it was that which she had last sung with him. When the last sad note had sadly echoed, the door opened, and Paolo entered.

His appearance cannot be described.

"Mademoiselle, I have come to say goodbye. You see that during these days I have not bothered you. This shall be the last time. Your father doesn't know that I am here; he wouldn't be terribly pleased about it. Therefore I am unable to linger. Goodbye, Ida, goodbye forever."

So saying, he took her hand and covered it with kisses... then he made a violent effort, and headed for the door.

"Paolo, stay a moment longer," murmured a voice behind him.

He came back, and sat down next to her.

Ida would have liked not to cry... but when she spoke her words were broken by sobs.

"I want to sing Weber's song to you for the last time," she said. "It is the song of farewell."

And with that voice in which there were tears, she began…

She was unable to finish. Halfway through she stopped and began to weep uncontrollably.

Only then did she understand how much she loved the one who was at her side.

Paolo had wanted to be strong, but now all his resolve abandoned him.

With one hand he grasped Ida's hand in his, while, shaken by an irresistible agitation, he encircled her waist with his other arm.

The poor girl abandoned herself. Her beautiful head bent like a flower laden with dew and came to rest on the young man's chest.

She had loved him for almost a year without knowing it—now she could no longer live without him.

How was it that their lips became united and took a long kiss?…

Those two hearts, which in the next moment would have to separate forever, beat each against the other, as if they were attempting to sink one into the next…

But suddenly her female instinct awoke; the terrible idea that she no longer belonged to herself flashed through her mind. Suddenly she understood the word *duty*—and forcefully released herself from his embrace.

Soon after she calmed down.—Then she became afraid that her father would come in, and Paolo left. He left almost happy. He was loved.

Ida had a fever all night and was delirious in a most peculiar manner; the doctor was called in. It was decided that it was better to delay the marriage.

The Marquis came to pay her a visit and let it be known that he was extremely pained by such a cause for delay.

But she did not want to.—She got up, saying that she was fine.—She put on the sumptuous wedding dress covered in lace sent from Paris; she let the bridal crown be set on her head, and as white as her dress, with a steady gaze, with a sure step, she was led to the altar.

The Count then understood, despite himself, that she was not a bride, but a victim that the altar had to receive. And yet he wanted to continue to delude himself, and thought that the magnificence of Sentis Castle and the noisome amusements of Paris life would soon enough make her forget everything.

It is difficult to give an idea of the affection that the Count felt for his daughter. She was everything to him. A relic of a dead century, he had remained alone, without friends (most of them were no longer alive, or had passed into the ranks of other parties), and Ida, the living image of her mother, the only woman he had ever truly loved, was the single scope of his existence.—He was frightened by the fixed gaze she had that morning.

The ceremony was brief. Ida pronounced the sacramental "yes" in a steady voice, and came out of the chapel arm in arm with her husband with that same step, and as pale as when she had entered.

Her thoughts were confused. The pain was gone. She felt her head becoming light. A joyless smile was on her lips. As she passed the large reception room, she remembered the place where she had fallen when she was five or six years from one of the high armchairs which she had climbed onto. Her eyes were fixed and a little glassy. She was no longer a woman; she was a beautiful statue that walked.

On earth, all was over for her. The first joy had fled, the last hope had disappeared. Now her reason was beginning to waver. The shock had been so strong, the effort she had made to overcome herself so violent, the repugnance she felt for the bond she had taken was so great, that moment of love that she had been unable to resist had revealed to her with such painful evidence how strong her passion was, the delirium of the night had so verily agitated her, that in the face of the horrible reality of her sacrifice, everything had become confused and dark. In those days she had suffered more than she had realized, and the effect of that suffering now struck her fiercely. When the hour of the wedding had been set and the days followed one another with their relentless speed, it seemed to her that fateful time was passing with a vertiginous rapidity and she felt a sense of painful helplessness in not being able to stop it. But however much one has the sad certainty of reaching a sad destination, until it is actually reached, a faint ray of hope continues to stubbornly rest on our path—but, once the destination has been reached, faced with undeniable reality, it also fades and leaves one in the dark.

She was continuously smiling—and the Count was terrified by that smile. She answered randomly, and stammered incoherent words. She was calm and quiet, but her mind seemed to have darkened. One might have feared that madness, that horrible specter, was waiting to swoop down on her.

Allow us a parenthesis. These types of madness, which come between the final hour and the grave to take hold of those who have fought in a single hour the entire struggle of a lifetime, make the thinker stop and doubt. In fact, are these deliriums true deliriums? Or are these not instead, at the last moment, the fading away of human nature, the wisdom of a new life that in this life appears as madness? Has the eye that no longer clearly distinguishes earthly things been blinded by an invading darkness, or has it instead been blinded by the light of heaven?... Those incoherent words that the mouth speaks but which are not understood, are they empty of meaning and devoid of reason—or, instead, are they not understood simply because they are the very first syllables of another language?...

But let us return to poor Ida. In the hall, she received the congratulations of the guests in a distracted manner, but her fictitious strength was diminishing from moment to moment and she felt herself succumbing to an effort too great for her. She had to succumb. She retired to her room and, fully dressed as she was, with orange blossoms on her head, lay down on her virginal bed.

The Count, very worried about the state of his beloved daughter, left the guests, abandoning them to the groom's brilliant conversation, and ran to Ida's room. He found her calmer, but always with that fixed gaze and that ominously sweet smile.

"Leave me be," she said, "I want to sleep."

And in fact she soon fell asleep. When he saw that she was dozing, he kissed her on the forehead and tip-toed out.

She slept for more than an hour, in a heavy, dark slumber.

When she awoke, she was unable to bring any of her thoughts together and it seemed to her that she had lost her memory; she only recalled that she had suffered greatly. Then, abruptly, she put her hand to her forehead as if she had suddenly remembered something. She got up and, with a slow and smooth step, left the room.

She traversed the large rooms, the gallery, the corridors, and entered the green room.

She sat down at the harpsichord and, accompanying herself, sang the song by Weber.

Her voice almost seemed to no longer belong to this earth.

After a moment, the whole room was impregnated with those notes...

On her way out she met Paolo.

She did not seem to see him, despite the fact that she was staring at him with her large eyes that were full of a mysterious light.

He took her hands, and covered them with kisses.

But she withdrew them and, bursting into a convulsive laughter that echoed oddly between the old walls, she said in a broken voice:

"Do not touch me, sir—I am the Marchioness di Sentis."

The unfortunate girl could no longer pull herself together. She fell ill and the illness was of long duration, and although not painful, was without remedy.

The care of the doctors, the prayers, the solicitude of paternal affection, it was all useless. There were a few hours of hope in the midst of the days of sorrow, but they, alas, were soon extinguished! Everything possible to save her was tried, but the illness was inexorable.

She was one of those who, when dashed against the passions, are broken, and die. In the delicacy of her youth, her emotional state was closely linked to her physical state. Finally, her long agony came to an end. The village curate and the Count were kneeling by her bed. A little further back stood the Marquis di Sentis.

She had a moment's respite and spoke a little. Her words were incoherent and strange, but affectionate towards her father.—She kept repeating Paolo's name.

Her last words were: "Let me sleep." So saying, she leaned her beautiful head back and closed her eyes.

II.

Three days later, the village church was decorated sumptuously in black and silver.—A crowd of villagers were kneeling on the steps.

On a large placard, surmounted by the Montsauron coat of arms quartered with that of the di Sentis, was written in white letters on a black background:

TO THE SOUL
OF THE NOBLE LADY
IDA DI MONTSAURON
MARCHESA DI SENTIS
Taken
On Her Wedding Night

By a Sudden Sickness
Leaving the Groom Bereaved
And the Father Inconsolable
God Give Eternal Rest
And the Crown of Paradise.
R. I. P.

Nothing remained of that angel who had passed from the earth but a pompous twelve-line inscription.

The interior of the church was imposing. Funereal torches illuminated it with a severe white light. In the same way as without, it was draped in black and silver. In the middle stood the little coffin on which a garland of flowers was placed.

The suffering of the old Count was terrible and frightening. Not a single tear fell from his eyes—but in two hours he seemed to have aged ten years.—He had wanted to preside over everything related to the funeral himself, so that the last of the Montsaurons would be buried honourably. He attended to the obsequies in the gallery of the house. Then he accompanied the procession to the family tomb. She was placed near the Countess di Montsauron. On the gravestone only her name was written, with the date of birth and that of death.

After fulfilling these agonizing offices, the Count went on foot, accompanied by the Marquis and the priest, to the outskirts of the village, where a mail coach was awaiting him.

"There, where Ida died," he said, pointing to the old house, "I no longer wish to stay."

The Marquis had offered to accompany him, but he had refused. He did not want anyone with him, except his old valet, who, also sad, climbed up on the back of the coach.

The Marquis and the curate, with their hats in their hands and his faces troubled by strong emotion resolutely endured, sustained him as he got into the coach.—He shook their hands and shouted to the coachman:

"To Paris!"

The heavy coach moved forward and the four horses left at a gallop. The Marquis di Sentis returned to his lands in Normandy.

Paolo never found consolation for Ida's death—but he did not die of it. Time and art are great comforters. He left for Paris where before long he made a name for himself.

The one whose suffering was truly immense was the old man. A great, distressing suffering.

This alone is left to speak of.

III.

Five years have passed since the events we have narrated.

In the hotel of a small village, in an ugly, low-ceilinged room, covered with wallpaper that was red half a century ago, a white-haired gentleman with a wrinkled face and a curved back is sitting in a large armchair, and seems absorbed in his thoughts. Let us hasten to say that this old man is the Count di Montsauron, otherwise he would certainly not be recognized. The Count was in excellent health and had a very strong constitution; this alone had saved him from following his daughter to the tomb; for the pain which had struck him was one of those which often kill;

losing her, he had lost everything that kept him here on earth.

We have previously seen how he endured the terrible blow. And, as has already been said, he had not felt himself capable of returning to those walls where Ida had given her last sigh, and had left for Paris. There he tried to distract himself, but in vain. After some time he bought a small villa on the delightful banks of the Seine, and had a moment of hope that a peaceful life, in a pleasant and beautiful place, far away from the scene of misfortune, could gradually close the wound that was still bleeding. He spent two months there, but actually, day by day, the solitude increased his gloomy melancholy.—So he decided to travel.

And here began the supremely sad spectacle of that old man who journeyed and journeyed, fleeing his sorrow. He travelled all over Italy and Spain, and everywhere he found nothing but the image of his dying daughter—and her last words and her last glance were heard and seen always.—In vain he ran from those thoughts that followed him like phantasms: it seemed that they had incarnated within him.

Furthermore, little by little, despite himself and although he tried to fight it, a new feeling took hold of him.

A new evil was gnawing at him, a greater evil that was added to the other: remorse. The horrendous thought that, in the death of Ida, he was not innocent, slowly, bit by bit, invaded his mind, and once and having taken hold, never left him a moment's peace. He was certain that she had died of sorrow. And in the marriage with the Marquis he had not forced her, but also... Sometimes he woke up at night with a start and seemed to see his Ida in the middle of the room still dressed as a bride, but already pale with her final pallor. He had never been superstitious; and yet there were now times when he was afraid to be alone.

We find him again—five years later—tired of travelling. One fine day he had felt an extremely violent and rather strange desire. Just as, directly after the misfortune, he had wanted to flee his old house, so now he experienced an intense longing to return. The melancholy that had followed him everywhere was now redoubled by this new feeling (which many perhaps would not understand), which might be called the nostalgia for suffering. Not being able to forget, he wanted everything to speak to him of his misfortune; not wanting to console himself, he found an acrid voluptuousness in drinking the cup of bitterness to its last drop. He longed to see the room where she had died and to lay flowers on her grave. Tired of everything, he wanted to drown himself in his affliction.

This was why he made the return journey with the same celerity that, five years earlier, his departure, which resembled an escape, had been affected.

By instinct and by nature, by education and conviction, the Count was eminently religious. And although he had sought the comforts of religion, that too had been in vain. All the consolations that were given to him to alleviate his pain were of no avail. It was a sad thing that at his age, even his faith had abated!

Superstition took its place.

All that he had heard told in the long course of his life related to supernatural stories, those anecdotes of ghosts and phantasms of which we have all heard our share, he now remembered and they agitated and disturbed him. It seemed as if they were all being repeated to him; and truly—though he did not want to confess it—it was not without concern that he was thinking of the first night in his large room, so grave with its yellow *lampas* tapestry and the vaulted ceiling with its gilding tarnished by time.

This, however, did not diminish in the least the intense desire to go back within those walls where his daughter had passed away—and the dread, which he wanted to shake off, but which he still had, of nocturnal apparitions, a dread derived from remorse, which only increased his desire to be in the old house again. He had, so to speak, the curiosity of fear; he wanted to see what might happen to him.

When we found him again, therefore, he was sitting in a large armchair in that ugly hotel room, immersed in his sad thoughts. Having arrived at that last station of his return journey, pushed on by that feverish impatience that was to suffer again where he had already suffered, agitated by a tremendous curiosity, he had decided, despite being exhausted, to spend but a single night there and leave the next day.

And so it was that the next morning Antonio, the old servant, entered his room.

"Monsieur Count," he said, "the horses are harnessed and all is ready."

"It's unnecessary," the Count replied. "I will not be leaving today."

The following day it was the same. Finally he gave the order that there would be no departure until further notice.

We sometimes have gloomy warnings that seem to come from above. The presentiment puts itself in our path and points towards the abyss. The Count, knowing he was just a few leagues from the sumptuous family tomb where his Ida rested, was already feeling from that closeness an occult thrill. The fear of the supernatural became stronger every day and turned into terror.

All in him was a contradiction.—He wanted to see his old home, but dreaded it. And this fear was tripled by the presentiment that weighed on him and it overwhelmed him.

So he remained for around fifteen days in that ugly hotel and could not resolve to leave. He was like a man who is scared of opening a door.

One night he had a dream. It seemed to him that he was near his daughter's tomb; but it was transparent and she was waving her arms, and despite her closed eyes, her pale face was radiant. The expression on her face was one of an ineffably sweet sadness.

He was gravely moved by that vision. He felt grieved and full of remorse at the sweet melancholy impressed on the face of his dead daughter. And the desire to see that tomb again became more vigorous than the fear of ghosts. In fact, although at the bottom of his soul he still had an indestructible, arcane fear, it was no longer apparitions that he was afraid of. What did he fear then? He no longer knew. He had seen Ida now and that vision had not been a nightmare, but rather almost a comfort. Yet he still felt that vague and indefinable terror, and perhaps, since it was secret and unknown, he felt it even more so.

But his desire to see his home again over-
came all.

There was no longer any procrastination.
His impatience suddenly became manic. He
got up, ordered the horses, hurriedly and hastily made his preparations and half an hour later
the heavy carriage was already rolling along the
postal road.

It was sunset. On the terrace of the old house
servants and peasants and with them Ida's
maid were gathered together. Everyone was
eagerly extending their gazes towards the road.
A very animated whisper meandered among
the groups. Why had everyone come? It was
due to a servant who had claimed to have seen
from the window a carriage on the postal road.
It looked like nothing more than a black dot;
but it was heading for the house.—Everyone
knew that the Count was soon to arrive, and
the sight of that carriage therefore provoked
great emotion.

"It seems to me as if it will never get here," the gardener finally said. "Maybe it won't be him."

He had not finished saying these words, when he saw the Count's carriage, black and covered in dust, appear at the end of the magnificent drive. The horses, although they seemed tired, covered with sweat and foam, galloped bravely up to the terrace.

The carriage came to a halt.—It was, for those assembled, a moment of unspeakable emotion. Everyone felt a shiver go through their bones.

The moment was solemn.

Their old master, who was so dear to them, who they had seen flee, struck by that terrible blow, the death of his only hope, they now saw return after a five-year absence, which they well knew had been but a futile attempt at soothing his pain.

The window opened and the Count looked out, and wavered for a moment.

It seemed like a last hesitation.

How he had changed!…

Finally he stepped down and, bent over, supported on both sides, he slowly climbed the terrace steps.

Everyone had rushed to meet him, kissing his hands, the tails of his coat, holding him up… In an unsteady voice he thanked them.

When he entered the hall, two silent tears were seen rolling, slowly, so slowly, down his cheeks.—For the first time since Ida had died he was crying.

He walked on into the large dining room, where he found the table already set. He dined, with everyone serving him—talking with everyone, thanking everyone, asking for news about what had happened in his absence. He was quite pleased, after all, to find himself in the old house; he congratulated himself on having had the courage to come.

He then retired to his bedroom, and he lay down.

When he was alone once again, for the first time in a great while in his large and rather severe room, he could not keep back a moment of fear. Yet he ended up falling asleep, and his slumber was not disturbed in any way.

So, to be brief, a month passed without anything extraordinary happening to him. He had, furthermore, been many times in the room where Ida had died, had laid his old head on that pillow where the poor bride had exhaled her last sigh, had wept like a child, since by now he could weep, but nothing had happened to him.

He had walked around the silent rooms, the long galleries, the corridors, but had seen nothing unusual or supernatural. His apprehensions, his superstitious fears began to diminish. But he was not afraid of apparitions: Ida had appeared to him and smiled at him. And yet where did that restlessness, that presentiment that he felt so strongly, come from?

One day he was coming out of the library and saw that a door which ordinarily remained closed, was open. It led to a long corridor, which extended to the left wing of the house. At the end of the corridor was the green room, which we know, the pianoforte room, poor Ida's favourite place. The thought flashed on him that, since his return, he had not yet been there. It probably was a matter of habit, since even previously he had not made it a custom to go there.

It was a place beloved by his daughter; he who only still breathed for that sacred memory immediately felt tempted to enter it. He passed through the long corridor, and leaning on his cane (which he was now never without), he headed for the green room.

He moved along, bent over, his eyes dull and head down. The sadness he felt in his heart was stronger than usual. He pushed the door open and went in.—Immediately his superstitious fears overwhelmed him. Even though it was broad daylight, he was trembling more now than at night in his own gloomy chamber.

Everything in the room was in its place, everything was as it had been when Ida had last set foot in there. After that day, no one had entered. The antique harpsichord was open and on the music stand could be seen an open piece of sheet music. It was the song by Weber—the favourite song that she had recited so many times with Paolo, the one that had made them fall into each other's arms and exchange that long kiss of love that was their only moment of happiness; the last one she had sung, with her gaze fixed, her heart broken, in an accent of inconsolable pain, in a voice that was no longer of this world.

That sad melody of love had echoed for a long while between the old walls. And when it had finished, the whole room had seemed as if it were impregnated with those notes...

Seeing that sheet music on the music stand and the harpsichord still open, the Count felt himself shudder.

Suddenly his cheeks were covered with a deadly pallor, his legs trembled, a sepulchral chill passed through his veins, and he had to lean on the harpsichord—holding on to it with both hands so as not to fall.

A very faint sound of music could be heard. The harpsichord, without being touched by any visible hand, was playing notes. It was a sad, sad motif; a sweet melody that seemed like the lament of a heart swollen with love...

It was the song by Weber.

And the notes, those melancholy notes which used to echo in that room, arose, arose with a heartrending phrasing which seemed to no longer belong to this life.

At first the voice was soft, faint, as if it came from afar, as if it was coming from beneath the ground.

To the father it seemed as if it was arising from the grave… and, seized with unspeakable terror, he held onto the harpsichord with all his might.

His premonition had come true: he no longer feared apparitions, but he knew that something awaited him. He now felt a horrible fear, but did not see any ghosts.

The voice swelled and it swelled and grew louder. It was like the roar of a storm, like a burst of tears, like a battle of the heart. And the notes succeeded one another, clear, distinct, strong, with an arcane accent, as if a hand that was both masterful and divine had touched the keys.

The Count's hands were trembling convulsively.

The sound continued. The singing took on the inimitable accents of celestial music. Artistically, the execution was the most splendid imaginable.

It was, in fact, an execution such as no mortal hand or human voice could ever hope to render. There was such a strange resonance in those notes, such divinely heartrending expression in those accents, that certainly if it had had to come out of a human breast, it would have broken it. It was one of those songs that one dies for.

All creations of art are but attempts; the artist never fully externalizes what moves them internally, never expresses everything they would like to. Here, however, Weber's whole mind was perhaps expressed. It was a new edition of his song, revised and corrected in heaven. It might be said that the angels had lent a hand. It was as if in those notes the rustle of their blue wings could be heard...

The song went on powerfully, intricate as the struggle of the elements; but the sad initial motif was always heard—seemed to seep through. That angelic voice, which resembled the voice of Ida, was heard among that divine tempest of notes.

The Count stammered incoherent words.

Finally, that gale, which had reached its peak and was like the thunder of a heavenly rage, began to gradually wane.

Slowly, little by little, it grew calm. And the initial motif, that sweet melody of love, which had always been heard despite all, now returned and became dominating.

The Count trembled. A deadly chill twisted through his body. His lips tried to pronounce a prayer. Finally, the motif was by itself once more, but now it was faint, as faint as the echo of another life.

Then, suddenly, the accents became so loud, so arcane, that it seemed as if the harpsichord would break.

The final notes were full of terrible sorrow.—They were the last cries of a soul that is being violently torn from their mortal remains by an overpowering wrong.

The old man felt his life failing him. The singing continued—an agony of notes.

Then the last one, lengthy, gloomy, sad, supernatural, vibrated with an accent that could not be imagined by a human mind. It seemed to come from the bowels of the earth and fly like an arrow to the heavens. It was the final cry, the cry of someone who dies of love.

In that accent, the Count seemed to recognize Ida's voice.

All of a sudden his hands lost all vitality and left the harpsichord, which he had been holding onto throughout that period of strange agony; as pale as he was, he quickly turned white and with a suffocated rattle, he collapsed on the floor.

That last note still echoed.

A PARTIAL LIST OF SNUGGLY BOOKS